Frog and Friends Save the Day

By Kristy Stark, M.A.Ed.
Illustrated by Guy Wolek

Publishing Credits

Rachelle Cracchiolo, M.S.Ed., *Publisher*
Aubrie Nielsen, M.S.Ed., *EVP of Content Development*
Emily R. Smith, M.A.Ed., *VP of Content Development*
Véronique Bos, *Creative Director*
Dani Neiley, *Associate Editor*
Kevin Pham, *Graphic Designer*

Image Credits

Illustrated by Guy Wolek

Library of Congress Cataloging-in-Publication Data

Names: Stark, Kristy, author. | Wolek, Guy, illustrator.
Title: Frog and friends save the day / by Kristy Stark, M.A.Ed. ;
   illustrated by Guy Wolek.
Description: Huntington Beach, CA : Teacher Created Materials,
   [2022] | Audience: Grades 2-3. | Summary: ""The tropical rain
   forest is being destroyed! A group of animals work together to
   save their home""-- Provided by publisher.
Identifiers: LCCN 2021052870 (print) | LCCN 2021052871 (ebook) |
   ISBN 9781087601878 (paperback) | ISBN 9781087631929 (ebook)
Subjects: LCSH: Readers (Primary) | LCGFT: Readers (Publications)
Classification: LCC PE1119.2 .S734 2022 (print) | LCC PE1119.2
   (ebook) | DDC 428.6/2--dc23/eng/20211117
LC record available at https://lccn.loc.gov/2021052870
LC ebook record available at https://lccn.loc.gov/2021052871"

5482 Argosy Avenue
Huntington Beach, CA 92649
www.tcmpub.com

ISBN 978-1-0876-0187-8

Printed in Malaysia. THU001.46774

Table of Contents

Chapter One

The Ground Rules

"Let's get started," Posey says calmly. The animals keep talking. *I guess I will have to try again*, she thinks.

Posey is a tiny frog with a big voice. "Let's get started," she says louder.

All the animals freeze. They look at one another, and then they look at Posey. All the animals are scared of her. They know that the poison dart frog could make them very sick if she wanted to.

"Sorry, Posey," says Jag. The jaguar is not easily frightened, but she *is* scared of Posey.

Posey starts again. "Good, I have your attention. Let me remind you of the ground rules for the meeting. No eating the animal next to you. No thinking about eating the animal next to you."

"Did you hear that, Jag?" says Cappy, a large capybara. He points to his eye patch. "I do not want to almost be your lunch again."

Jag rolls her eyes at the large rodent. "Run faster next time."

Posey clears her throat. "We have important things to talk about—our home."

Chapter Two

A Big Problem

Mack, a large macaw, speaks up. "I agree, Posey. Let's talk about what happened to our home. I didn't like moving."

"Neither did I," replies Posey. "These humans definitely have to be stopped. They can't just cut down trees in our forest. And then, they set fires! That is no way to treat anyone's home."

"Calm down, tiny one," says Jag. "Yes, we had to move, but it won't happen again."

Cappy responds, "I'm certain it was a one-time thing. We are perfectly safe now. My new dwelling is great because it's farther away from Jag."

Jag crouches as if she is going to pounce on Cappy. He flinches, and she smiles.

"I really like my new home," says Mack. "The tree has thick branches. My family and I are quite happy."

"Mack, you just said that you hated moving," Posey says. She shakes her head at Mack. "Make up your mind!"

Mack shrugs his wings.

"Don't worry so much, Posey." Jag walks away, and the other animals follow.

Posey sighs loudly. *I can't protect our home by myself*, she thinks.

Chapter Three

Trouble

Early the next morning, Posey hears voices. She opens her eyes and sees humans starting fires.

She quickly wakes Mack. "Wake up! Sound the fire alarm!"

He caws loudly to wake the other animals. They gather their families.

Jag says, "Over here, everyone! I found a good place for us to hide."

Jag finds a safe spot in a large area of brush, away from the fire. All the animals bunk together.

"Stay away from my family, Jag!" Cappy snaps.

Jag pretends to lunge toward him. Cappy jumps as he covers his family.

"Lucky for you, we already ate," Jag says, laughing. "We are too stuffed to have another bite."

Posey yells, "Stop it! We barely escaped another fire. This is not the time for jokes. We lost our homes again!"

"I'm sorry, Posey," says Jag. "We should have listened to you."

"Yes, I'm sorry too," says Mack. "How can we save the forest? We can't keep letting them burn it."

"I'm glad you're ready to listen. I have an idea," Posey says.

Chapter Four

Teamwork

The animals work together. At night, the nocturnal animals keep watch. "Pleasant dreams, Posey!" says Jag. "The big cats and I have this area covered."

"Thanks, Jag!"

During the day, the other animals watch over the area.

Several nights later, Jag spots people. She instantly alerts Mack. "Wake up! Humans!"

Mack quickly sounds the alarm. "This is not a drill! I repeat, this is *not* a drill!"

The jaguars form a circle around the humans. "On three," says Jag. "One, two, three!"

The jaguars roar loudly. The humans are scared, and half of them run away.

Some humans go deeper into the rain forest. "I'll get them!" hollers Cappy. He corners two men and charges at them. He runs up one man's back and launches onto the other. He uses his nose to poke the man in the eye.

"Got you!" says Cappy. The men run back to their truck and hurriedly drive away.

A few other men try to start cutting down trees, but Posey won't let that happen.

"Come on, frogs!" she yells. The poison dart frogs jump onto the men. The humans know that the frogs secrete poison. They look at the frogs and scream.

"Oh no, poison dart frogs! Let's go!" one man shouts.

The men shake off the frogs and leave the rain forest.

Chapter Five

Safe at Last

"Great job, everyone!" Posey says.

Jag approaches Cappy. "Great job, my giant rodent friend. I didn't know you could launch yourself like that."

Cappy smiles. "I'll do anything to protect our home, even work with you."

Jag lies down. "Cappy, I promise not to try to eat you again. I will hunt for meals in another part of the rain forest."

The other predators agree to Jag's promise.

Mack says, "Thanks for saving our home, Posey."

Posey responds, "I did not save it alone. We all saved our home. We couldn't have done it without one another."

About Us

The Author
Kristy Stark writes fiction and nonfiction books for kids. She loves to read mystery books in her free time, and she spends time hiking and being outdoors, too. She lives in California with her husband and two children.

The Illustrator
Guy Wolek has been an artist for over 30 years. He has done a variety of jobs with his skills, such as sketch artist, illustrator, and art director. Guy enjoys creating art.